W9-BEZ-186

Jingle BATS

A *novel by*

Sharon Jennings

HIP-JR.

HIP Junior
Copyright © 2007 by Sharon Jennings

All rights reserved. No part of this book may be reproduced or
transmitted in any form or by any means electronic, mechanical,
optical, digital or otherwise, or stored in a retrieval system
without prior written consent of the publisher. In the case of
photocopying or other reprographic reproduction, a licence from
CANCOPY may be obtained.

LIBRARY AND ARCHIVES CANADA CATALOGUING IN PUBLICATION

Jennings, Sharon
    Jingle bats / Sharon Jennings.

(HIP jr)
ISBN 978-1-897039-22-9

I. Title. II. Series.
PS8569.E563J56 2007   jC813'.54   C2007-901266-3

General editor: Paul Kropp
Text design and typesetting: Laura Brady
Illustrations drawn by: Kalle Malloy
Cover design: Robert Corrigan

1 2 3 4 5 6 7   11 10 09 08 07

Printed and bound in Canada

High Interest Publishing is an imprint of the
Chestnut Publishing Group

Sam and Simon get work as Santa's elves at a mall just before Christmas. Their boss is mean, Santa is a grouch, and then some toys start to disappear. The Bat Gang is being framed!

CHAPTER 1

All I Want for Christmas Is . . . Everything!

BRIIIIING! BRIIIIING!

The bell! School's out! Two whole weeks off for the holidays. Kids and teachers were yelling *Merry Christmas! Happy Hanukkah!* Yeah, yeah. Just get me out of here!

I grabbed my stuff and flew down the hall, down the stairs and out the door. My buddy Simon was a few paces behind me.

"Hey, Simon!" I yelled. I threw a snowball and made contact. A direct hit!

Simon cleaned the snow off his glasses. "You asked for it, Sam," he yelled back. Then he threw a snowball at me, and he missed.

"Nyah, nyah!" I said. "You throw like a girl!"

I knew that would make him mad. Simon and I both bent down for more snow. It would have been a good snowball fight, too, but then we heard our teacher's voice.

"Sam! Simon!" shouted Mr. Chong. "There's no throwing snowballs on school property!"

I looked all around. Then I spotted Mr. Chong hanging out the window. He'd been watching the whole thing.

"It's the holidays!" I yelled up at him. "Rules don't count."

"Detention first day back, Sam." Mr. Chong shouted down. "Even worse if you keep it up."

"Way to go, moron," said Simon.

Simon is my best friend. But not when he calls me a moron. So I pushed him face first into the snow. We wrestled around a bit until I got snow down my pants. Simon can't throw, but he's pretty good at wrestling.

Then we walked home, talking about the holidays.

"I'm doing nothing," I said. "I'm going to watch TV all day from now until Christmas. I asked for *Counter-Strike* for Christmas. So then I'm going to play *Counter-Strike* all day."

"Sure, Sam," groaned Simon. "What about shovelling? What about babysitting your sister? You think your parents are going to let you do nothing all day?"

I felt like shoving Simon into a snow bank again. I mean, he *is* my best friend, but sometimes he's such a nerd. I've known him almost four years now and he can really get on my nerves. Maybe it's because he's always right. But he did save my life a couple of months ago when I found a dead body in the graveyard. I mean, I found a dead body that wasn't supposed to be dead. Well, you had to be there for the whole thing to make sense.

"So what are you going to do for two weeks?" I asked him.

"I have to make some money," Simon answered. "I want to buy some gifts."

"For who?"

Simon gave me the moron look again. "For my parents, stupid. Maybe even you."

"Me? Really? Hey! I know what you can get me. I really want a . . . Wait a minute. Does this mean I have to get you a gift?"

Simon turned his back on me.

"Don't go to any trouble, Sam."

"Oh I won't. I don't have any money," I said.

"You mean you aren't even buying gifts for your family?" Simon asked.

But just then I had a brainstorm. I don't get too many and this one was really good.

"Hey!" I shouted. "You can do *our* shoveling *and* baby-sit Ellen! My parents can pay *you* and I can watch TV all day!"

What a plan.

Simon laughed. "You're such an idiot."

So I grabbed some snow and pushed it down his collar. Simon took off and dodged in front of a couple of little kids up ahead. One of those kids was wearing a stupid hat.

I'd know that stupid hat anywhere. It was my sister, Ellen. She was with one of her dorky friends. They were holding hands and skipping and singing a lame Christmas song.

So I crept up behind them. And then I started singing full blast.

Jingle bells. Ellen smells!
Her best friend laid an eggggggg!

Before I could start the next line, Ellen turned around and threw a snowball. It hit me right in the face.

Simon looked over and laughed. "Wow, Ellen! You throw like a girl! Can you teach me to throw like a girl? Your aim was perfect!"

I wiped the snow off my face and looked at them both. I didn't know which of them to chase first.

Simon took off around the corner to his house.

Ellen and her friend ran up the driveway to our house. "Mommy! Mommy! Mommy! Sam's after meeeeeeeee!"

My mom opened the door. Ellen and her dorky friend ran inside.

"Now what have you done?" my mom sighed.

I shook my head. "I didn't do anything. Ellen threw a snowball at me. A big one . . . and it hurt!" She had to believe me. I still had snow on my nose.

"Oh, Sam. Ellen's a little girl. How could she hurt a big boy like you?"

I had another one of my brainstorms. "Because she's not really a little girl, that's why. She's an alien wearing a little girl costume."

My mom shook her head. As I got into the house, she held up a flyer. "Speaking of costumes ..."

It was a picture of Santa with some elves.

"So?"

"It's an ad from the mall," my mom answered. "They're hiring kids to be Santa's helpers for a few days."

"So?"

"So I signed you up, Sam. I know you need money. I know you want to buy all of us gifts this year." Then she added, "For once."

"WHAT? You signed me up to be an elf?!"

"You start tomorrow at nine o'clock. Just like school."

I stood staring at the flyer. The snow on my nose began melting. I could feel my whole Christmas holiday dripping away.

But I knew my mom. There was no way out. For the next few days I was going to look really stupid. For the next few days I'd have to *work*! Too bad I didn't get killed a couple of months ago. Too bad Simon saved my life. This was all his fault!

Then I had another brainstorm. I walked over to the phone and dialed the number on the ad. I spoke to some lady for a minute and then I said, "Oh yeah, and my best friend Simon McDonald wants a job too. He'd just *love* to be an elf!"

No way I was going down alone.

CHAPTER 2

Here Comes Santa Claus

This stupid teenage girl held out our costumes.

"I'm not wearing that," I told her.

"You have to, loser," the girl snapped at me. Then she pointed to the left. "There's the men's change room. I suggest you use it."

Pretty nice boss, eh?

Simon and I went into the change room. When we came out, we were wearing green tights, green shorts, a green shirt, a red apron, and a hat with bells on it. Oh yeah . . . and shoes with curly toes.

If anyone saw us, we were doomed.

"Where are your ears?" asked the girl.

"Uh . . ." I pointed at my head. "Duh."

The stupid teenage girl stamped her foot. "Not *your* ears, loser. Your elf ears."

Simon went back into the change room. "Here they are," he said. He pulled something out of a bag. Then he stuck these huge pointy things over his own ears.

I thought I was going to pee my pants laughing.

"I don't get paid to listen to you laugh," the girl told me. "Now put yours on, loser."

I grumbled to Simon. "We'd better be making lots of money," I said. "If I have to look this dumb, I want to be rich."

The stupid teenage girl shot me a nasty look. I noticed that she had a nametag – Tara. That's "a rat" spelled backwards. It seemed to fit.

"Now listen. You make seven bucks an hour," Tara told us. "You work eight hours a day. You work the five days left until Christmas and you'll make a lot of money. Just figure it out."

"Hmmm. That's seven times eight times five. So that's ... um ... that's ... um...."

"Two hundred and eighty dollars!" Simon shouted.

"Show off," I said.

But two hundred and eighty dollars really is a lot of money. No way was I spending all of it on gifts for my family. I wanted lots left over for me!

"When do we start?" Simon asked. "What do

we do?"

I wanted to kick him. "You don't have to be so keen, moron," I whispered to him.

"You don't have to be so snotty, Sam," he shot back.

We followed Tara down a hallway to the main mall. At the same time, we saw Santa coming toward us. For a moment, I forgot how old I was. Santa! Wow! Then I got a grip. Santa was just some old geezer dressed up.

"Hi, Santa," said Simon. "You look like the real thing!"

Santa glared at him. "Who are you, kid?" he asked.

How dumb was that? Couldn't the guy see our costumes?

"Duh," I answered. "We're your elves."

Santa grabbed my ear. I mean my real ear, right through the fake ear. Then he shook me.

"Wise guy, eh? Listen. This job is hard enough. I don't need any smart-mouth kid messing up my gig. Got it?"

I rubbed my ear and nodded. We all headed off to Santa's Castle in the very center of the mall. Something smelled really good. I looked around and saw the North Pole Bakery right behind us. An old, fat lady dressed up as Mrs. Claus was baking cookies. Suddenly I was starving.

Santa went over to his throne and sat down.

"What's with him?" I asked Tara.

She rolled her eyes. "All the Santas are like that. They think they're superstars. They grow their hair and beards all year just to get jobs at Christmas."

I looked over at Santa. "You mean his beard is real?"

Tara nodded. "Just wait till some little brat pulls it. You'll find out."

I rubbed my sore ear. I couldn't wait until some kid yanked Santa's beard.

"Tara, do you work here all the time?" Simon asked.

She nodded. "I take the job every Christmas. I need the money for college, so I put up with it. It's lousy, but it's only for two weeks."

"But if it's for two weeks, how come we're just being hired now?" Simon asked. "I mean, there's only five days left."

"We had two other elves before you. They were fired." Tara drew her finger across her throat.

She started to walk away, but Simon grabbed her arm. "Can you at least tell us what our job is?"

Tara shrugged. "Yeah, I guess. It goes like this. After the parents pay me for the photo, you keep the kids in line. Then you bring the kids up to Santa one at a time. And then you have to make sure they behave like good little girls and boys for the photo. Oh, yeah, if they make a donation, you put it in the toy box."

"What donation?"

"To the toy drive for poor kids. If they donate, they get a big discount on the photo." Then Tara walked away. Maybe she wasn't a rat after all.

"Doesn't sound so hard," said Simon to me. "I wonder why the last two elves got fired?"

"Maybe they made Santa mad," I said. "Maybe they tried to test out his beard."

Just then, Santa stood up and yelled. "You, elves! Get your butts over here! The mall's going to open in one minute. Hurry up!"

Simon and I ran over to the castle.

Santa wasn't finished yet. He grabbed both Simon and me and pulled us close. "Now listen and listen good. Don't let any rotten kids near me. Understand? Some dumb kid pulls my beard or pees on my lap and you'll wish you were dead. Got it?"

Simon and I nodded. Then Santa let go of us.

I was glad I didn't believe in Santa any more. I didn't want a creep like this coming down my chimney!

CHAPTER 3

'Tis the Season to Be Jolly!

I thought it would be easy at the start, but I was wrong. People were lined up outside the doors, waiting for the mall to open. Then they rushed in and headed for Santa's Castle.

"Out of my way!" shouted one mother.

"I was here first!" shouted another.

They each had two kids and soon everyone was pushing and shoving. I saw Santa glare at me, so I got to work.

"Hey! Knock it off!" I yelled. "It's Christmas. Ho, ho, ho, and all that crap."

Simon pushed me aside. "Idiot!" he hissed. "You're supposed to be an elf, remember?" Then he hurried over to the line.

"Shhhh! Shhhh!" Simon said to shush them. "Remember, Santa knows if you've been bad or good."

The kids got quiet right away. But the parents were something else.

"What's your name?" one of the moms asked Simon. "I'm going to report you to the manager."

"For what?" he asked.

"For being rude to a customer," she barked at Simon.

That's when I came to Simon's rescue. "Aw, come on, lady," I said. "He just asked your kids to get in line and be nice."

"And I'll report you, too. What's your name?" she demanded.

I had another brainstorm.

"I'm Comet and he's Cupid."

The mother looked ready to smack me, but just then Simon got her kids up on Santa's knee.

"Ho, ho, ho!" said Santa. "What beautiful children! Let's smile for Santa. Ho, ho, ho!"

"I don't wanna smile!"

"I want cookies!"

Simon ran over and did a little jig. It's a goofy dance that makes him look like an idiot. But the jig worked. As soon as the kids started laughing, the cameraman took a photo.

Santa pushed the kids off his lap. The little boy ran over and kicked me in the shins.

"Ow! Ow, ow, ow!" I yelled and did a jig of my own. The other kids in line all laughed.

Then the mother handed me a bag. Inside was a strip of stickers.

"What's this?" I asked.

"My toy donation. For the discount."

Was she crazy? She got a fifteen dollar discount for a ten cent gift?

Tara saw me staring. "Just put it in the box," she whispered. "We get all kinds here. Some people are

really cheap, but there's nothing we can do."

I walked over to this huge box. It looked like a big, fancy gift. And it was empty.

"Where are all the toys?"

"We clear them out of here every night," Tara answered. "To keep them safe."

"Safe? Why? Do the cheapies show up and steal their toys back?"

24

Tara shook her head, and then Santa began to yell. "Hey kid! Are you paid to work or to stare into space? Get your butt over here!"

So that was pretty much the whole morning. Simon and I got the kids to sit on Santa's knee. I stopped the kids from pulling on the old guy's beard. Simon danced around to make them smile. And we took the donations over to the box.

A lot of the donations were great. Some parents showed up with cool board games, like Monopoly and Life. Or giant puzzles or sports stuff. One dad donated lots of computer games. I even saw *Counter-Strike* in the donation box. Now that would be a great gift!

But other parents were worse than the first mom. One lady handed me a pack of gum. I said thanks and started to open it. "It's not for you, stupid," she yelled at me. "It's for the poor kids."

At twelve-thirty, Tara told us to take off for lunch. It was about time. I could smell cookies all morning from the North Pole Bakery, and it was driving me nuts.

"You've got half an hour," Tara said.

"No time to change," Simon said. "Let's grab a slice."

"In these clothes? Are you nuts?"

"Who cares, Sam? It's Christmas. We're elves. We're making money. Let's go."

I was tired and I was hungry, so I followed Simon to the food court.

Big mistake.

A group of girls from our class were eating fries. They saw us right away. How can girls giggle so much? Oh yeah. They're girls, that's why.

"You two are *sooooo* cute!"

"Oh Sam. You're *adorable!*"

I tried to ignore them. My idiot friend, Simon, just smiled. Then he showed them how he does his jig.

"Sit down and shut up!" I told him.

But Simon ignored me. He told the girls all about our job. Could this get any worse?

Yup.

"I know!" said one dumb girl. "Let's all go get

our picture taken with Santa and his elves! It'll be *sooooo* cute!"

Oh right. Just what I needed. Photo proof of looking stupid!

CHAPTER 4

You'd Better Watch Out!

I grabbed Simon by the apron – apron! Sheesh! –
and hauled him out of the food court.

"Why do you do these things to me?" I yelled at
him. "Now all the kids at school will know about
us."

"So what?" Simon replied. "Get a grip, Sam.
We've got jobs. We're making money. So what if
we're elves? I think it's cool."

"Oh really?" I said. "Cool. You think it's cool to

wear tights and pointy ears." I shook my head. Sometimes Simon really is a loser.

"Oh, come on, Sam. We *are* cool. The girls said so."

"Have you lost your mind?" I asked him. "They said we're *cute*. Not cool. *Cute*. It's a big difference."

"Who cares? They like us."

"You *have* lost your mind," I shouted. "Who cares what the girls think?" I gave him a hard look, and then I grabbed him by the shoulder and shook him. "Why are you so interested in girls all of a sudden? You don't . . . I can't even say it. You don't . . . *like* them, do you?"

Simon didn't answer. He pushed me and grabbed my hat. Then he ran with it through the mall, singing "Jingle Bells" at the top of his lungs. I chased after him. And I started thinking, maybe I need some new friends.

We made it back to the Castle only a minute or two late. Santa didn't yell at us because he wasn't there. But Mrs. Claus was. She came over with a tray of cookies.

"Fresh from the oven," she said.

We grabbed two each.

"Gee thanks, Mrs. Claus," said Simon.

The old lady winked at us. "Don't tell anyone. A couple of cookies for Santa's little elves."

We thanked her again and watched her waddle off.

"I think she's been eating too many of her own cookies," I said.

"Shhhh!" Simon hissed. "She'll hear you."

"I mean it. She's really fat."

Then Tara came over, eating a cookie. "See that line of kids? Entertain them."

"Huh?"

"You heard me," Tara ordered. "Keep them happy till Santa gets here."

So Simon started singing "Frosty the Snowman" and I hummed because I couldn't remember the words. Then he did his dorky dance and I sort of thumped around behind him. Some of the kids started crying. The parents all looked really tired.

"Ho! Ho! Ho!"

We all turned to watch Santa enter the Santa Castle.

I led the first kid up to Santa's knee. Oh great. Santa was covered with snowflakes and he stunk of cigarettes. So that's what Santa does at lunchtime. Sneaks outside to smoke. Nice.

The mother handed me a big bag of toys. "Thanks," I told her. "This is great."

I went over to put it in the box.

But the computer games weren't there.

I leaned way, way over and pushed stuff around. I saw all the other stuff, all the board games and puzzles and everything. So where were the games?

"Simon," I hissed. "Come here."

As soon as Simon got the next kid on Santa's lap, he came over with a bag of books.

"The computer games are gone," I whispered. "Look."

Simon stared into the box. "Maybe they were put somewhere to be safe."

"Why not put away all the rest?"

Simon shrugged. "Nothing else costs that much."

"I don't care. I'm going to ask . . ."

"Hey!" It was Tara yelling at us. "You two planning on working today?"

We ran over. I wanted to tell Tara about the games, but kids were going nuts in line. So we worked for over an hour non-stop.

And then it happened.

Santa jumped up and shouted. A boy went flying off his lap.

"Look at me! My pants are soaking wet. Why isn't this ankle-biter wearing a diaper?"

Santa stalked off as a mom ran to pick up her son.

Tara shook her head. "Now what?" she groaned. Then she turned to us. "Get up there and sit in the big chair. Maybe some parents won't mind a photo with Santa's elves."

So Simon and I ran up to the throne. Some parents left the line. But some looked so tired they didn't care. Soon Simon and I had kids on our knees, smiling for the camera.

"I hate this job," I whispered to Simon. "I can't do four more days. I'll die."

"Maybe we'll get paid more," Simon said.

Just then some kid jumped up on me and landed where it really hurts. Then he tried to pull my ears off.

I grabbed the kid's arms and twisted them behind his back.

"Smile, you little creep," I hissed at him.

So of course he began to howl. I let him go and he stomped on my foot.

"We'd better get paid more. No way I'm putting up with this!" I told Simon.

Then I heard a deep voice from up above. "I told you it was a hard job."

I looked up to see Santa standing over me.

"Yes, sir," I gulped. Simon and I ran back to the line of kids.

The first dad in line gave Simon a huge teddy bear. Simon thanked him and went over to the donation box.

I led a little girl up to Santa. I noticed he had changed his pants. I guess a mall Santa has to have a few extra pairs, just in case.

I looked up to see Simon hanging over the side of the toy box. What was he doing?

Then Simon stood up and I saw his face and I knew what he was doing.

He was looking for a toy that wasn't there.

CHAPTER 5

He Knows If You've
Been Bad or Good!

If that wasn't bad enough, guess what happened next!

"Simon! We're here!"

Oh great. The girls showed up, just like they promised.

Simon ran over to them.

"Get in line," he said. "I'll make sure you get a great photo."

"How much is a photo?" asked one girl. I think her name was Carla.

"Twenty-five dollars without a toy. But only ten dollars if you make a donation," Simon told them.

"What donation?" Carla asked.

"Duh. Can't you read?" I pointed to the sign. "You have to donate a toy to a poor kid. Then you get a discount."

Five girls looked in their purses. Then they put their heads together.

"We have enough money for a photo with the discount," Carla said. "But we don't have enough money for a toy."

"Tough. Get lost," I told her.

Carla rolled her eyes. "You're a creep, Sam." Then she looked at Simon. "Can't you help us out, Simon? Get us some kind of discount? Please? You're so adorable."

I wanted to gag. "No, he can't help you out. Rules are rules."

"Pleeeeeeeeze, Simon?"

I could see Simon felt bad. He knew the rules, but because he liked some dumb girl, he was ready to cheat. What a loser!

Then I had another brainstorm.

I pointed to one girl's shopping bag. "What's in there?" I asked.

"Why?" she said.

"Are they Christmas presents for someone?" I asked her.

"No, nosy. They're for me."

"Why don't you donate them to Santa's gift box? Make some kid real happy."

"Because they're for me, you jerk."

"Too bad," I said. "Move along. You're holding up the line."

She ran over to her stupid friends. At last, a couple of girls pulled out some make-up, and a hat and mittens set. Carla brought them over.

"Simon, is this all right?" she asked.

"That's great," he gushed. "I think you're wonderful."

"And I think *you're* wonderful, Simon," she said. I was about to vomit when Carla looked over at me. Then she stuck out her tongue.

So I left Simon to pose with his new fan club. Tara took their money and I took the donations over to the box. I saw what Simon had seen earlier. All the board games and the sports gear were gone.

I got really mad. I don't even know why. Why should I care if stuff got stolen? It wasn't *my* stuff.

But I did care. Maybe it was just because I was working so hard. But maybe I felt sorry for some kid with no presents on Christmas morning. I mean, that would really stink.

So I marched over to Tara. "Why are some of the gifts missing?" I demanded.

"What are you talking about?" she asked.

"The games, the teddy bears. They're not in the box. But all the cheap stuff is still there."

Tara went over to the donation box. "Oh no! Not again."

"You mean this has happened before?"

She nodded. "This happened just the other day. And we never found the gifts, either. They were stolen."

"Did you call the cops?"

"Yup. They couldn't do much," Tara replied.

I left her and went back to Simon. The dumb girls had left so I could tell him what was going on. We worked a couple more hours and took turns watching the gift box. But nothing else went missing that afternoon.

But a couple did the next day. Some guy had given a bunch of music store gift cards. Gone. So were a really neat backpack, a doll and a few DVDs.

We never saw it happen. We saw the stuff go in the box, but we never saw it come out.

At last, the day was over. Santa stood up and waved at the kids still in line.

"Ho, ho, ho. Santa has to go," he said.

Simon and I left, too. We went to the change room and dumped the elf stuff in our locker. We were just heading outside when I remembered my key. My folks were going to a party, so I needed a key to get in the house.

"I'll catch up," I told Simon and ran back into the mall.

I hurried into the change room and put the key in our locker. I pulled the door open.

At the bottom of our locker was a doll and a teddy bear. The *stolen* doll and teddy bear.

CHAPTER 6

He Sees You
When You're Sleeping

I slammed the locker door.

I turned around fast. Did anyone see me? Nope. I was alone in the change room.

Think fast! Think fast!

The stuff wasn't in our locker twenty minutes ago. So someone waited till we were gone. Then he put the toys inside. But why?

Well, duh. *So Simon and I would look like the thieves*, I said to myself. We'd get blamed. And then we'd get fired.

Then I got really mad. I ran over to the door and looked up and down the hall. No one was there. I went back to my locker and grabbed the stolen toys. I had to get rid of them. I looked all around the change room. Nowhere to hide them.

Brainstorm! I tip-toed down the hall. Then I peeked into the women's change room. It was pretty fancy. There was even a sofa and a couple of chairs. I checked under the doors of all the stalls. I was alone. I shoved the toys under the sofa. Then I took off.

Simon hadn't waited around for me. Moron. So I caught the next bus and went home. My parents and Ellen had already gone out. They left me a big bowl of soup. Ugh. I dumped the soup and grabbed a frozen pizza. Then I phoned Simon. No answer.

I phoned Simon every ten minutes. Still no answer. Where was he?

Simon still wasn't home at eleven. His parents must have dragged him out somewhere. But I had to tell him about our locker. So I wrote him a note in Bat code.

This is a really easy code. You just change the vowels around.

A E I O U Y

Y U O I E A

So my name, Sam, would be Sym. But then you write it backwards – mys.

Tnugre! Nulits sait no rei rukcil. Doh muht no 'slrog nyc. Tyhw it id?

I hopped the backyard fences to Simon's house. Then I stuck the note under the front door. I ran back to my place, slipping twice in the snow. Why didn't I wear my boots? And why wasn't I wearing my coat? Maybe my mom is right. Maybe I am stupid.

A snowball hit my window after midnight. I knew what that meant. I waved to Simon and hurried outside.

"Where have you been?" I whispered. I was only in my pajamas, so I was freezing.

"My parents took me to visit some aunts. They're kind of nutty, but I got some really cool gifts," he answered.

I started to ask Simon about his gifts but then

Hid them in girls' can. What to do?
Urgent! Stolen toys in our locker.

46

stopped. I wasn't freezing my buns off for that. So I told Simon about the stolen toys in our locker.

"So what do you think?" I asked him.

"I think we're being set up," Simon replied. "Someone's stealing the toys and wants it to look like we did it."

"But why?"

"To take the heat off the real thief," Simon told me. "If there's a search, the toys would be found in our locker. We can say we didn't do it, but who'd believe us?"

I thought for a minute. "And you know what? Not all the toys were in the locker. Just a couple. The thief kept the really good stuff, but we'd get blamed for all of it."

"Yeah. And meanwhile, all those little kids get nothing for Christmas," said Simon.

I got really mad. "Why don't we go to the cops? They know us. We've caught crooks before. They'd believe us."

But Simon shook his head. "I want to catch the jerk who's doing this. Red-handed. We've done *that* before, too. We just have to think of a plan."

"Well ..."

But then the porch light came on. My dad came outside.

"What are you two doing out here?" Dad said. "It's one in the morning! And Sam, why are you in your pajamas?"

Then my dad stopped talking and looked at both of us hard.

"You're up to something, aren't you?" Dad said.

"No, Dad. It's just that, well ... Simon was out tonight. And we wanted to talk and ..."

"Huh! I know you two. And I know you're planning trouble. It's a good thing you're both working. At least you can't get into trouble at the mall."

I just rolled my eyes at Simon.

CHAPTER 7

Making a List, Checking It Twice!

I sneezed a few times and wiped my nose on my sleeve. "Remind me to wear a coat next time."

"No problem," Simon replied. "Wear a coat next time."

"Thanks. So what's the plan?"

"We'll take our breaks at different times," Simon said. "That way one of us is always watching the gift box."

"What if someone complains?" I groaned. "What if Santa yells at us to get to work?"

"If Santa complains, then maybe it's him," Simon answered.

"Santa? You're joking!" I said.

"Why not Santa? He's pretty weird."

"Yeah, and Tara's pretty mean. I hope it's her," I said. Any girl who keeps calling me a loser might just steal toys from a toy box.

We got to the men's change room and went inside. I stared at our locker. The lock had been broken. I suddenly felt really sick. Simon opened the door. Our elf stuff was there but nothing else.

"You ready?" Simon asked.

"Sure," I lied.

Simon went out to the hallway. He started yelling for Tara real loud. "Tara! Tara! There's a thief! Help! HELP!"

Tara came running from the mall.

"What's going on? Stop yelling," she yelled at us.

"Someone broke into our locker," I yelled back.

Tara stopped yelling. "Oh. Yeah. Sorry about that. Some more toys were stolen, so security busted into your locker."

"Why?" Simon demanded.

Tara shrugged. "It was the first two elves who got caught with the stuff last week. We found some toys in their locker. They got fired. So security just figured it was you. They broke your lock, but there was nothing there. That's all. No big deal."

"No big deal," I repeated. Hah! No big deal to her, but what about us? What about our rights? If I were a lawyer . . .

Tara shook her head. "Now put on your ears and get to work."

Tara left us and we got changed. But I wasn't happy about all this. I always thought Tara was a stupid teenage girl. Now I *knew* she was a stupid teenage girl.

"You know what Sam? I bet those first two elves didn't do it. I bet they were set up like us. They got fired for nothing."

I nodded. "And you know what else?" I said. "The person who did it must be really mad at us. He planted those things in our locker, but I screwed up his plan."

Simon nodded. "So maybe the guy will do something really stupid. Maybe he'll act without thinking, just to get us in trouble."

I agreed. "So we have to be careful."

We got dressed and went out to Santa's Castle. But Santa wasn't happy to see us.

"So you're back? Didn't steal enough stuff yet? But don't you worry. Santa's got his eye on you," he said.

"We didn't steal anything," replied Simon.

"Yeah," I added. "And *we've* got our eye on *you!*"

Santa clenched his fists and started toward us. But just then Tara yelled at us to get ready. The mall doors had just opened up.

The lineups were crazy. The kids were nuts and the parents were wild. Everybody wanted photos with Santa.

So we worked all morning and never took our eyes off the box. Good thing, because people were donating good stuff. One guy even gave a *Star!* hockey stick. Sure wish I had one of those. Maybe I

could buy myself one with the money I was making. Unless I got fired.

At break time, we took turns running for junk food. But at lunchtime, we ran into a problem. Santa's Castle shut down for a half hour, so we both had to go for lunch at the same time.

"You go," I said to Simon. "Bring me back a pizza slice and I'll stay here."

"I'll hurry," answered Simon.

No one noticed that I stayed behind.

Except for Mrs. Claus. She waddled over from her shop with a couple of cookies in her hand.

"Tsk, tsk, tsk," she said. "You boys work too hard. Won't they even give you a lunch break?" She gave me the cookies.

I smiled at her. "Thanks for the cookies. But don't worry about me, Mrs. Claus. My friend's getting me something to eat."

"You're a good boy," she said.

Mrs. Claus smiled at me and went back to her shop. I ate the cookies, but I was still starving.

I went over to the donation box to look at the hockey stick again. But there was a problem. The hockey stick wasn't there.

Then there was another problem. Someone grabbed me by the neck and spun me around.

"Caught you this time, punk."

CHAPTER 8

Gonna Find Out Who's Naughty and Nice!

I twisted and turned. Santa held on with hands of iron.

Then I remembered.

I yanked on his beard . . . and it came off!

"Hey! You said this was real!" I yelled.

Santa shoved his face into mine. "You're dead meat, turkey!" he yelled in my face. His breath was none too pleasant.

So I stomped on his foot, and this time he let go. Then I ran down the steps of the castle.

"Stop that elf!" Santa yelled behind me.

I looked up and saw the cookie shop. *Mrs. Claus!* I thought. *She'd believe me! She knew I didn't steal anything. She was with me. She had been watching me.*

I ran across the mall to her shop. People stopped to stare, but no one grabbed me.

"Mrs. Claus! Mrs. Claus!" I panted.

And Santa was right behind me, yelling, "Stop! Thief!"

Mrs. Claus looked up and saw me.

"Help me!" I cried.

Mrs. Claus came out from behind the counter. Then she looked up and saw Santa. He kept yelling, "Thief! Thief!"

And then Mrs. Claus turned and ran the other way. She didn't waddle. She really took off! She was running almost like a track star.

What? Where was Mrs. Claus going? I needed her help.

So I ran after her. And then I saw the silver blade sticking out from under her long skirt. What the . . . ?!

Santa was closing in. I kept chasing Mrs. Claus. So when the hockey stick landed in front of me, I tripped over it and fell.

Santa grabbed me from the back and hauled me to my feet. "Hurry! After her!"

"Huh?"

He didn't answer me. But now he was chasing

Mrs. Claus. So was I. Then I saw Simon coming back from the food court.

"Simon! We've got to stop Mrs. Claus!" I yelled.

Simon was shoving some pizza in his face, but he looked up and saw all of us running. Quickly, he dove for Mrs. Claus as she charged past him. She knocked him over, but Simon grabbed her hair. And it came off!

Simon lay there holding a curly, gray wig in his hand! Then he jumped up and followed us.

I caught up to Santa and rushed by him. I couldn't believe how fast Mrs. Claus could run. How could someone so fat move like that? And no one bothered to help us. They stood back and pointed and laughed. I guess they thought we were some special show for Christmas.

I chased Mrs. Claus into a store and out again. Then into a smaller store, and she was trapped. She picked up a pile of stuff on a table and flung it at me. It was ladies underwear! Yuck! I shook myself like a dog. I had ladies underwear all over me!

Mrs. Claus put her head down and roared into

me. She sent me flying through the air. I could feel myself flying up and back. Then I landed in something soft.

Yuck! More underwear! And it was slippery. As I tried to get up, I grabbed on to Mrs. Claus's dress. Then I heard something rip. Mrs. Claus kicked me as she ran past, but I kept holding her skirt.

Her skirt!

It was really thick and really heavy. It was lined with lots of pockets. And the pockets were filled with stolen toys.

I looked up just in time to see that Mrs. Claus was really a skinny bald guy. He raced out of the store. . . . and straight into Simon's arms.

"Gotcha!" cried Simon.

The bald guy struggled, but then Santa came up behind him. In no time, Santa had the bald guy in handcuffs.

Simon looked over at me and laughed.

"What's so funny?" I demanded.

"You've got a bra on your head."

CHAPTER 9

Santa Claus Is Coming to Town!

So it turned out that Santa was a cop. Tara was just a stupid teenage girl. And Mrs. Claus was really Fred Snert, or Baldy to his friends. He had been working the malls for years. He always got a job as sweet old Mrs. Claus, so no one thought he was a crook. Baldy had a trick skirt and he could hide just about anything under it. Anything but a hockey stick.

"I told you she was too fat," I said to Simon. Then I sneezed.

"You did," he said. "Want a Kleenex?"

We were sitting in the security office. They gave us cookies while we waited for the police.

"So how come you're here?" Simon asked the Santa cop. "Did you have a hunch Baldy was up to something?"

"This mall was hit really bad last year," Santa answered. "So we always planned to put an officer

64

undercover this year. I got sent to catch the thief. We didn't know it was Baldy."

"Why did you have to be such a grouch?" I asked. "Simon and I thought *you* were the thief."

"I hated this job," he replied. "It's too hard being a Santa. Little kids are terrible. I'd rather go undercover in a drug gang. At least those guys show you some respect."

"But did you really think we were the crooks?" Simon asked.

Santa shrugged. "I wasn't sure. A couple of years ago we had a gang of kids working the malls. We caught those guys, but you could have been a new gang."

"A gang? There's only two of us," I said. Then I remembered. "What about the first two elves? Did they really steal stuff?"

"They said they didn't. But we found toys in their locker," Santa said.

So I told him about the toys in *our* locker. And I told him where I put them. Someone ran to the women's change room to get the doll and teddy bear.

"I bet those kids got framed, just like us," said Simon.

"We'll check into it," Santa said.

Just then, the door flew open and Tara came in. "Come on, you guys. There are a million kids lined up out there. You've got to get back to work."

"Not me," said Santa. "I'm done here."

"That's what you think," Tara said. "You can't leave me alone with all those brats. Until a real Santa shows up, you've still got a job."

"I'm a cop, not a Santa."

"Please," Tara begged. "I need the money for college. It's only for a couple of hours."

Santa – the cop – looked a little surprised. "Oh, what the heck," he said at last. "So long as no kid pees in my lap."

So we all trooped back to the castle. Simon and I did our thing. Santa put on his beard and did his.

The next day, there was a new Santa. The new Santa was really nice to us. He even let me pull his beard to see if it was real. With this Santa, it was.

"You boys are heroes," the new Santa said. "Lots

of children will be happy because of you."

Yeah. And the mall owners were happy, too. They took our picture and posted it up all around the mall. "*Elves Catch Christmas Crook!*" They even gave us each a gift card to spend at any store.

So in the end, we made a lot of money. I bought some CDs for my parents. I got the kind of sappy music they like. I also bought a big doll for my sister, Ellen. And I still had lots of money left over for me. But I didn't spend it all on myself, after all. I bought a computer game and a teddy bear for the toy drive. I put them in the donation box.

Please don't tell anyone.

Oh, yeah. I bought Simon a present, too. The lady in the store wrapped it up real nice for me. Here's what I wrote on the card:

Arrum Symtsorhc, nirim.
Upih uht ucyl suotnyp tof.
Fo tin, uvog muht it reia dnuorflrog.
ih, ih, ih!

Be sure to read the other BAT GANG novels

Bats Past Midnight

by SHARON JENNINGS

Sam and Simon wonder about a fancy car that hangs around their school late at night. When they try to find out more, they end up in trouble at school, at home and with the police.